# The Whispering Town

For Will, Lizzy and Sophie. You are in my heart. Always and forever. — J.E.

To Giulia and the publisher who have always believed in me. — F.S.

KAR-BEN PUBLISHING
A division of Lerner Publishing Group, Inc.
241 First Avenue North
Minneapolis, MN 55401 USA
1-800-4-Karben

For reading levels and more information, look up this title at www.karben.com


Library of Congress Cataloging-in-Publication Data

Elvgren, Jennifer Riesmeyer.
    The whispering town / by Jennifer Elvgren ; illustrated by Fabio Santomauro.
      pages   cm
    Summary: In Denmark during World War II, young Annet, her parents, and their
  neighbors help a Jewish family hide from Nazi soldiers until it is safe for them to leave
  Annet's basement.
    ISBN 978-1-4677-1194-4 (lib. bdg. : alk. paper)
    ISBN 978-1-4677-1196-8 (eBook)
    1. Denmark—History—German occupation, 1940–1945—Juvenile fiction. 2. World
  War, 1939–1945—Denmark—Juvenile fiction. 3. Jews—Denmark—Juvenile fiction.
  [1. Denmark—History—German occupation, 1940–1945—Fiction. 2. World War, 1939–
  1945—Denmark—Fiction. 3. Jews—Denmark—Fiction.] I. Santomauro, Fabio, illustrator.
  II. Title.
  PZ7.E543Whi 2014
  [E]—dc23                                                    2013002195

Manufactured in the United States of America
2 — CG — 7/1/14

# The Whispering Town

Jennifer Elvgren

Illustrated by
Fabio Santomauro

KAR-BEN
PUBLISHING

"There are new friends in the cellar, Anett," Mama said when I woke up. "Time to take breakfast down to them."

I paused at the top of the stairs. The cellar scared me because it was dark. But the whispering voices gave me courage.

When I reached the bottom, I entered the secret room where we hid Danish Jews from the Nazis. A woman and her son sat on a cot.

"I'm Anett," I said, holding out the basket. "Mama made you breakfast."

"I'm Carl." The boy took the basket and handed his mother a roll and a soft-boiled egg.

"We thank you," she said.

Back upstairs, I sat down to my own breakfast. "How long will our new friends stay?" I asked.

"Two nights," said Papa. "On the third night a boat will take them to Sweden."

"While they're here, we'll need more bread." Mama said.

After breakfast I walked to the bakery.

"We have new friends," I whispered to the baker.

"Here is extra," he whispered back, handing me a bulging bag. "Stay safe."

On the way home, I saw Nazi soldiers knock on a door across the street.

Even though they had been in my town for a long time, my stomach still knotted when I saw them.

"Mama, Papa, soldiers across the street!" I said when I came home.
Mama tapped three times on the cellar door to warn our friends to be quiet.

After the soldiers left, Papa looked up at the cloudy sky.

"No moon tonight," he said. "It will be difficult for our friends to find the harbor in the darkness."

The next day, I took food to the cellar again. Again I let the whispering voices guide me down the dark stairs.

"This will help the time pass," I said, handing Carl some library books.

He took them and smiled. "I love to read."

"Mama, I need new books," I said, when I came upstairs.

After breakfast I walked to the library.

"We have new friends," I whispered to the librarian.

"Be careful," she whispered back, handing me extra books.

On the way home, I saw Nazi soldiers knock on our neighbor's door.

"Mama, Papa, soldiers next door!" I said when I came in the house.

Mama tapped three times on the cellar door.

After the soldiers left, Papa looked up at the cloudy sky.

"No moon again tonight," he said. "Maybe the clouds will clear tomorrow."

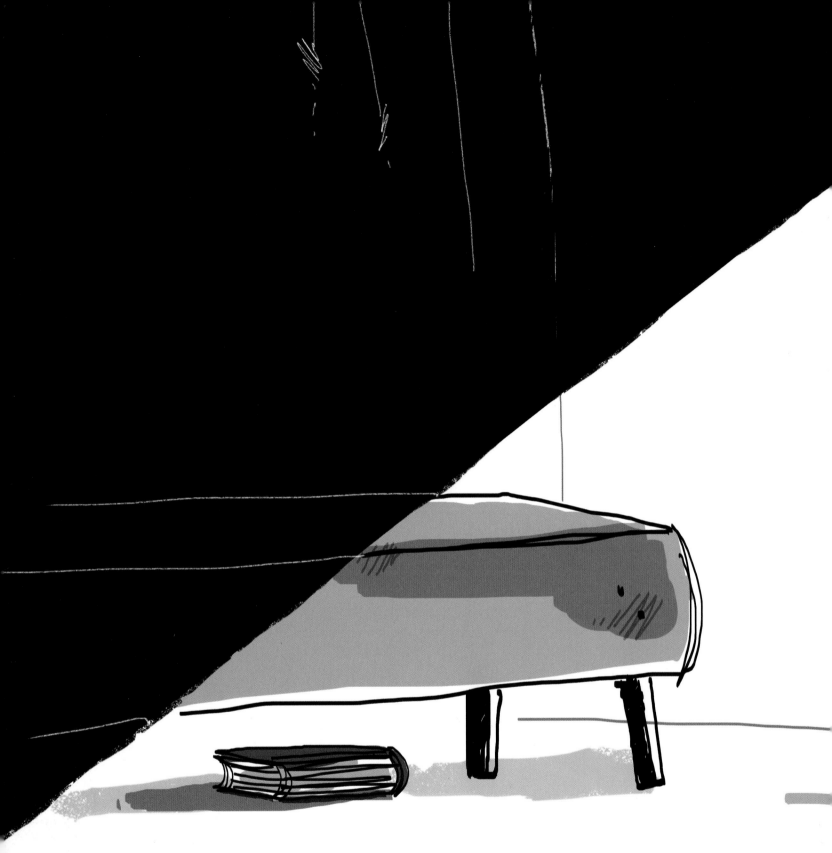

Again, the next morning, I let the whispering voices guide me down the dark stairs.

As Carl reached into the breakfast basket, a heart-shaped stone fell to the floor.

Carl picked it up. "I found this with my papa the last time we walked on the beach," he said.

"It's beautiful," I said.

"Anett, we need more eggs," Papa said, when we finished breakfast.

I walked to the farm.

"We have new friends," I whispered to the farmer.

"Wish them well," he whispered back, giving me extra eggs.

On my way home, I saw Nazi soldiers heading for our house. I cut across the alley and raced through our back door.

"Mama! Papa! The soldiers are coming to our house!"

They didn't answer me. No one was home.

I tapped three times on the cellar door.

Then I heard pounding on the front door.

"BOOM. BOOM. BOOM."

I opened it a crack.

"We've heard rumors that someone is hiding Jews on this street," said a soldier, pushing the door open.

"I haven't heard any rumors," I said, trying to stop my voice from shaking.

"When we find them, we will arrest everyone," warned the other soldier.

Trembling, I closed the door.

"The soldiers were here," I said, when Mama and Papa returned. "They are looking for hidden Jews."

"Brave Anett!" Papa hugged me. "Our friends must leave tonight even though it is cloudy. How can we get them safely to the harbor?"

I thought about being afraid of the dark cellar, and how the whispering voices guided me down the stairs.

"Papa, what if people stood in their doorways and used their voices to guide our friends to the boat?" I suggested.

Papa stood quietly, considering my idea.

"That might work," he said. "Help me to arrange it."

I ran to the baker , the librarian , and the farmer to tell them about our plan. They agreed to help spread the word around the village.

At midnight, Carl and his mama came up from the cellar. Carl pressed the heart-shaped stone into my hand. "Remember me always, Anett."

I held the little heart against my own.

After Carl and his mama slipped into the night, I leaned as far as I could out my bedroom window.

I heard our neighbor whisper from his doorway. "This way," he said, guiding Carl and his mother toward the harbor.

Then our neighbor's neighbor whispered, "This way."

The whispers continued from neighbor to neighbor, until Carl and his mama had safely reached the boat.

I squeezed the stone in my hand and imagined them walking free on the beach in Sweden.

## AUTHOR'S NOTE

Less than a year after World War II began, Germany invaded Denmark. It would serve as a "buffer" to protect Germany from British attacks. Adolf Hitler also wanted the country's fertile farmland.

At first, the Germans allowed the Danish government to continue ruling. But as time passed, the Danes grew tired of the Nazis and began to sabotage the occupation.

By 1943, the Nazis could no longer ignore the Danish resistance and took over the government. Shortly after, they began to round up the estimated 8,000 Danish Jews and send them to concentration camps.

Danes hid Jews in private homes, warehouses, barns, hotels, and churches. Then they secured boats and hired fishermen to transport them across the sound to nearby neutral Sweden. Almost all of the Jews were smuggled out of Denmark.

About 1,700 Jews escaped from the small fishing village of Gilleleje. One moonless night, the town's citizens stood in their doorways and whispered directions to the harbor.